Maybe I Will Do Something

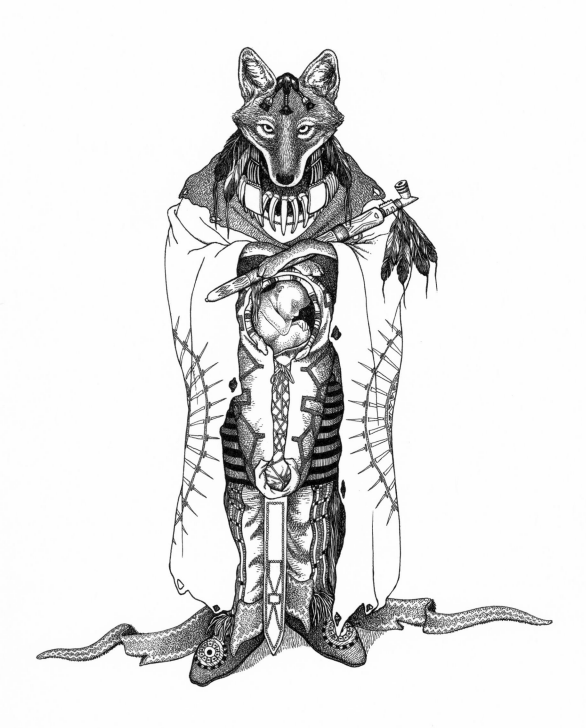

Maybe I Will Do Something

❖ ❖ ❖

Wayne Ude

Illustrations by Abigail Rorer

Houghton Mifflin Company
Boston 1993

Library of Congress Cataloging-in-Publication Data

Ude, Wayne.
  Maybe I will do something : seven Coyote tales / Wayne Ude ;
illustrated by Abigail Rorer.
      p.   cm.
  Summary: A collection of stories about the mythic Native American
trickster Coyote, based on traditional versions of the tales.
  ISBN 0-395-65233-2 : $14.95
  1. Indians of North America—Legends.   2. Coyote (Legendary
character)—Legends.   [1. Coyote (Legendary character)   2. Indians
of North America—Legends.]   I. Rorer, Abigail, ill.   II. Title.
E98.F6U34   1993   92-29392
398.24′52974442—dc20 CIP
                    AC

Printed in the United States of America

VB   10   9   8   7   6   5   4   3   2   1

This one is for Zachary Ude, and also for Kari Lynne Bailey, Brad Bailey, Jerry Olsen, and Jinny Olsen.

— W.U.

Contents

❖ ❖ ❖

Coyote's Cave   1

Coyote and Sun   11

Coyote Learns a Lesson   21

Coyote's Carving   29

Coyote and the Crow Buffalo-Ranchers   35

Coyote's Eyes   41

Coyote's Revenge   53

Afterword   71

Acknowledgments

I'm deeply grateful to those Native Americans who have told trickster tales, of which Coyote tales are only one type, and to those many persons, Native Americans and others, who have written down those tales.

Other than from the tales themselves, my earliest conception of Coyote as a trickster probably owed most to the work of collectors Paul Radin, Franz Boas, and George Bird Grinnell, and writer Jaime de Angulo. Many other writers have also influenced me, but twenty years ago, when I wrote my first three-paragraph Coyote tale, those four were most important. Marie Campbell and Zdenek Salzmann of the University of Massachusetts at Amherst also gave me valuable guidance when I was a graduate student there.

Finally, and most of all, I hope the people of Harlem, Montana, and of Fort Belknap Reservation, who told me all kinds of tall tales as I was growing up, will find these tales enjoyable.

These stories take place in the early days of the world, but not quite at the very beginning. In fact, there seem to be few Indian tales of a "very beginning." Traditional American Indians tend to see time as something circular, so that the world has no real beginning and won't ever end — though it can go through transformations so complete as to seem as though the old world ends and a new one replaces it.

So this story begins when the earth already exists beneath the water somewhere. Coyote and Wolf also exist, as do the diving animals. In fact, probably all *the other animals are alive somewhere; they just haven't come up out of the earth yet.*

Since these stories begin in the very early days of the world, Coyote and the others have to learn how things work. Certainly, they don't know very much to start with. In fact, they aren't even sure where they are or how they got there, much less what powers they have, or how to use them. They're a little confused at first — but then, Coyote is always a little confused, even today.

Coyote's Cave

❖ ❖ ❖

Coyote and Wolf had floated on a raft for days and days without ever sighting land, or any other rafts, or anything swimming in the water. They were puzzled: neither could remember what they might have been doing before they found themselves on the raft. That didn't much bother Coyote, who often couldn't remember, or so he thought — he couldn't be sure, because he couldn't remember whether there had been things to remember. Wolf, however, was sure that his memory, unlike Coyote's, had always been keen and reliable, though he couldn't remember anything before the raft, either. So Wolf concluded that this raft floating alone on endless water must be the very first thing that ever happened: this must be the very beginning of the world, and he and Coyote must be, so far, the very first beings in the world. Wolf was rather proud of himself for figuring all this out, so he didn't wait to tell Coyote: "This is the beginning of things, and we're the only beings in the world!"

All that was fine with Coyote, but he wanted to know what things this raft was the beginning of. Wolf couldn't tell him, though he thought there should be something. Maybe under all that water there might be earth, Wolf thought, but he wasn't sure he could swim, so he suggested Coyote dive down and bring back a handful — if Wolf had a little bit of earth, maybe he could do something.

Coyote looked over the side at the deep blue water, tasted it — salty! — and said he didn't think he could swim either. They would need someone who could dive for a job like that.

Just then, though he was sure they'd been alone just a moment before, Wolf noticed Loon swimming alongside. So Wolf asked Loon if he could dive. Loon laughed — Coyote envied that laugh, and set out to imitate it, until Wolf told him to be quiet so Loon could answer. Loon said yes, he could dive, and Wolf asked him to go down and bring back some earth. "Just a little bit," Wolf said, "that's all we need, if this story goes on the way I think it might."

Coyote wanted to ask what Wolf would do, but Wolf hushed him and they waited for Loon to come back up. "I don't know what we'll do if he doesn't make it," Wolf said. Coyote replied that they'd just have to send down one of the other divers. Wolf was about to ask, "What other divers?" when he noticed Duck, Porpoise, and a lot of others, floating and swimming around the raft. "How'd you do that?" he asked Coyote.

"How'd I do what?" Coyote replied.

"Never mind," said Wolf, "I think I see Loon, but he's sure swimming slow," and they all peered into the water.

"He doesn't look like he's swimming at all," said Big Turtle, whom no one had noticed alongside until just then. "I think maybe he's in trouble."

Wolf was about to ask Big Turtle where he'd come from when Loon floated to the surface and lay there, face down in the water. Big Turtle pushed him up onto the raft, where Wolf and Coyote jumped up and down on his chest until Loon got tired of that and came back to life.

Loon didn't have any earth with him, but he'd dived deep enough to see some farther below. So the other divers tried, but most came back in about the same shape Loon had, except for Porpoise. He made it to the bottom and up again all right, but he didn't have any claws with which to carry some earth. He'd tried to balance some on his nose, but it washed off. About the time Coyote and Wolf were ready to give up on the whole thing, Big Turtle said all right, he'd go.

This Turtle was a funny-looking fellow — had a shell on his back, and flippers where his feet ought to have been — but Wolf and Coyote were getting desperate by then, so they said, "All right, hardback, go ahead." They were a little irritated, and a little more scared, so they weren't being very polite.

Big Turtle was gone a very, very long time, and finally, he, too, came floating back up unconscious; but he had a tiny bit of mud clutched in his claws, and a little bit more caught in the grooves of his shell. When the other divers pulled Turtle over close to the raft to revive him, Wolf was able to gather enough earth to make a very tiny ball, so small that he could hardly see it. Coyote couldn't see it at all, though he said he could; but he was looking in the wrong place, and Wolf didn't believe him.

"Well," said Coyote, "it isn't very big, is it? We can't very well get out of the raft onto that, can we?"

"Well, no," Wolf had to admit. "We can't get on it yet. But maybe it will grow bigger."

They sat for a day or two, Wolf watching the tiny ball of earth, and Coyote sometimes watching Wolf and sometimes watching the place where Wolf said the tiny ball was. Then Coyote began to be bored and started muttering.

"What's that?" said Wolf, pretending not to hear.

"I said," yelled Coyote as loudly as he could, "that it needs to be larger! It needs to be larger, that's what I said! Larger, I said, larger —" He broke off because just as he said "larger" for the fourth time, the earth ball began to grow, and Coyote could see it. Until then, he'd wondered if Wolf were playing some kind of trick on him.

The earth ball grew quickly. First it filled Wolf's end of the raft so that he had to get over to where Coyote was, and then it pushed them both off into the water, where they learned they could swim a little bit after all. They paddled around for a while, trying to climb onto the ball as it grew, and grew, and grew, and finally they managed to get up out of the water onto the land, which was almost as wet anyway.

Right away Coyote began to complain, "Everything's wet and uncomfortable! We're up to our knees in mud! We were better off on the raft!"

Wolf told him to shut up. "Soon things will dry out."

"Well, I wish they would hurry up; that they'd hurry up, that's what I wish; hurry up, I said, hurry up!" After the fourth time Coyote spoke, the earth was dry and beginning to turn green with the first grass and the first small seedlings of what would be trees, but Coyote wasn't much interested in that.

"I'm hungry," whined Coyote, but Wolf ignored him, and the swimmers had stayed in the water where they didn't have to listen to Coyote. "I'm *hungry*," whined Coyote again, "I'm hungry, I'm hungry, I'm hungry!" But no one paid any attention to him because that's what Coyote always says, probably because it's always true, and saying it again wouldn't change anything.

Coyote complained louder and louder, and soon he was dancing up and down, crying at the top of his voice for food. "There should be food! There should be food! What sort of a world is this? There should be food! I said, there should be food!"

Just then, with a little *crack!* a cave opened in the rocks — some of the mud had dried so hard it had become rock — and ants began coming out, a whole long line of ants.

Coyote looked at the ants and said, "Maybe this is food?" He started licking them up; only some got by him so there could be ants in the world. Coyote thought this was a nice crunchy sort of food, though he didn't say so because then Wolf would want some and there might not be enough for both of them.

Ants aren't very big, and Coyote didn't think he would ever get enough. Soon Coyote began complaining again because other insects were coming out of the cave along with the ants and some of them weren't very good to eat — the stinkbugs he didn't like at all, and the bees stung his tongue when he tried a mouthful.

All this while Wolf was watching Coyote and laughing at him, though Wolf, too, was about ready to faint from hunger. Coyote was getting tired of working so hard for a meal, so he said, "These things should be larger! They should be larger! Larger, I said, they should be larger!" Then shrews, mice, rabbits, and other small animals scampered out of the cave.

Coyote had begun to figure things out, though he wasn't sure if it was the yelling, or the dancing, or saying things four times that worked. He didn't want to give anything away to Wolf, who was still watching him pretty closely, so he kept quiet and let the small animals pass by. Wolf advised Coyote to try a rabbit, but Coyote said, "No, rabbits look stringy," and ever since they have been.

After a while, Coyote got tired of watching rabbit and mink and muskrat and beaver and all the other small animals, so he yelled, "They should keep getting larger! They should keep getting larger! Larger, I said, larger!" Before long, antelope, deer, elk, and moose were coming out of the cave.

Wolf kept saying, "Come on now, let's take one of these."

But Coyote answered, "No, let's wait for something really big — I think I hear it now, so get ready," and they set themselves to jump on the next animal that appeared.

They could hear the next one rumbling up from underground long before it arrived. Coyote decided that he would jump the minute its nose stuck out, and he did. Only this time it was Grizzly Bear who'd come up to the surface. Grizzly roared when he saw Coyote leaping through the air at him, and Coyote almost died of fright when he saw Bear's teeth and hot red gullet. Coyote thought for sure he'd be Bear's dinner — but fortunately he didn't say it.

Instead he cried out, "You don't eat coyotes! You don't eat coyotes! Don't eat coyotes, I said, you don't eat coyotes!" Grizzly swatted him away and ran off into the trees which had been growing up all this time, where no one with any sense would bother him.

Coyote rolled end over end for a while, his nose tucked into his tail so it wouldn't get as badly bruised as the rest of him, and he had a long walk back. When he arrived, Wolf and his friends — those other wolves who must have come up out of the cave while Coyote wasn't paying attention — were still rolling around on the ground, laughing and howling out, "You don't eat coyotes! You don't eat coyotes! Don't eat coyotes,

I said, you don't eat coyotes!''

Then they heard another rumbling way down underground. This time even Coyote got out of the way until he saw what it was. The rumbling came closer, and Coyote saw a great shaggy head with horns approaching the cave mouth; he shrank back even farther, thinking of how good the ants tasted. "Watch out!" he cried. "This one has horns!" and he hid under a good-sized rock, with room even for his tail.

Then the buffalo ran out of the cave past all those who hid behind the rocks. Wolf started laughing again, but this time at himself and his friends. At the sound Coyote stuck his nose up from under the rock, decided it was safe, and climbed out.

Wolf spoke up then, "That's what I want to hunt!"

Even though Coyote hadn't seen this last animal very clearly from under the rock, he had seen those horns well enough and was certain this one was even bigger than the last, so he jeered at Wolf, "Hunt that? You'll have to hang around the edges and pick on the little ones, or the old and sick, if you want to hunt something that big!" He said it only once, so he didn't understand why Wolf kicked him. But Wolf had already figured out that while Coyote had to say big things four times to make them happen, smaller things also had a way of coming true even if he said them only once.

Wolf and his friends ran off then to hang around the buffalo herds and wait for there to be young buffalo, or old and sick buffalo. Coyote decided to go back to eating ants, or maybe chase one of those rabbits, which no longer looked quite so stringy. But first he stood in front of the cave and shouted, "No more! No more! We're running out of room for the big ones! No more, I said, no more!" He listened for a while, didn't hear anything else coming, and then trotted off to look for more ants, proud of himself for putting an end to the rush of new animals. There weren't any more to come after Buffalo anyway, as Wolf figured out later. But Wolf was still pretty upset that Coyote turned him into a hunter of the weak and old, so he kept quiet.

Coyote and Sun

After a while, the buffalo wandered off across the prairie, and Wolf and his friends followed them. Coyote moved into the cave all the animals had come out of, figuring it must be a fine, large place. It turned out not to be such a deep cave after all, and Coyote never could figure out how all those other animals got into it.

Coyote spent a lot of his time telling stories to any animals who would listen, mostly about how wise and important he'd been during the creation of the world. Even Coyote knows that stories are the way everyone comes to understand how the world works. Since the only stories the other animals knew were the ones Coyote told them, everyone agreed that he was the greatest person in the world. For a long time that kept Coyote happy.

Then the buffalo wandered back, staying for a few days to graze, and Wolf stopped by to tell Coyote about all the wonderful places he'd seen. There were other beings in the world, Wolf said, who hadn't come out of the cave or swum up to the raft. And one of them, Wolf said, was Sun, who lived in the largest and most beautiful tipi Wolf had ever seen.

All this talk made Coyote grumpy — especially the suggestion that Wolf wasn't the only being in the world that Coyote hadn't called up out of the water or the cave. He wasn't very pleased, either, that someone might have a tipi nicer than his cave, which he thought he had fixed up pretty well even though Wolf hadn't said anything when he came in to visit. So Coyote thought he'd better pay a visit to Sun's tipi and see if it was as large and wonderful as Wolf claimed.

Coyote said this wasn't the first he'd heard of this fellow, Sun, and maybe it was time he honored him with a visit. But he wasn't sure where to find Sun, who seemed to be pretty restless, always on the move when he wasn't hiding, so he asked Wolf how to find Sun's tipi.

Wolf said that depended on what time of day Coyote went looking: in the morning, the entrance to Sun's tipi was in the east, but in the evening it was to the west. That sounded funny to Coyote: Where was the rest of the tipi, then? Wolf said that *was* a question, wasn't it? Coyote agreed that it was a question, all right, but was there an answer to go with it? And Wolf said that Coyote had probably better go look at Sun's tipi himself if he wanted answers to questions like that. Yes, Coyote said, that's what he was trying to do, if he could just get a straight answer out of Wolf.

Coyote thought a little more about Wolf's directions and decided that he should set out for either the sunrise or the sunset. Remembering that he would always rather arrive at evening for the big meal and a good night's rest than at morning for a light breakfast and maybe even a day of work, Coyote decided to look for Sun's tipi at sunset. So he set off, heading west.

All day long Coyote trotted, using all four legs for a journey like this; he walked upright only for short trips. He kept the sun right overhead the whole way, figuring Sun would be heading for his tipi. And as the sunset glowed around him, Coyote saw at its center a tipi that must be Sun's. It was a new thing for Coyote, trotting through the sunset instead of watching it way off on the edge of the world — even Coyote himself glowed with all the sunset's bright colors. Coyote liked his new bright coat. Though he didn't think he'd want to wear it all the time, the colors seemed fitting for a person as important as Coyote to wear during special times.

From outside, the tipi didn't look like much to Coyote. It was large, but Coyote had seen large tipis before, he thought, though he couldn't think of any offhand. A tall, handsome, bright-faced fellow who must be Sun came out and invited Coyote to come in. Since this fellow Sun was standing upright, Coyote stood upright too and walked into the tipi. The entrance wasn't so large; Coyote could almost get through without ducking, though Sun had to bend a good ways to follow.

Inside, the tipi didn't look so big either, except that when Coyote looked hard at any part, the wall seemed to fade away and he couldn't quite see where it ended. Yet any part of the tipi he didn't look at directly seemed very close. Well, thought Coyote, probably that was what had fooled Wolf into thinking this was such a large tipi. Unlike Wolf, Coyote was too smart for such tricks.

Sun brought fresh water in a gourd and a bowl of fresh cherries, and invited Coyote to rest and refresh himself while Sun scared up something for dinner. Coyote said a polite thank-you and appeared to settle himself into the cushion Sun had given him — it was a thick, comfortable one. But Coyote thought maybe he'd follow Sun, see if he could learn how Sun hunted. Surely Sun must have some great power: What game could hide from him?

So Coyote crept along behind, watching. Soon Sun came to a clump of brush and stopped, laughing. "I know you're in there, you deer," he said, and he put on a pair of leggings he'd been carrying, embroidered so they seemed to be on fire. Then Sun began to dance around the brush, and as he came around for the fourth time he had his bow in hand, arrow ready. The brush burst into flame and deer came running out every which way. One ran right at Sun, who brought it down with a single arrow.

Then he set to work butchering the animal, and called out, "Hey Coyote, quit hiding back there and come help carry your supper!" Coyote, looking a little ashamed — because while Coyote doesn't mind what he does, he does mind getting caught at it — came from behind the rock where he'd thought

Sun would never see him. "You see, this is how I hunt," Sun said.

Coyote thought those leggings were the most beautiful things he'd ever seen, and useful, too. They'd look wonderful on the wall of his cave, and then Wolf wouldn't think Sun's tipi was so much nicer. That night, after they'd eaten and gone to bed, Coyote, who'd watched carefully to see where Sun hung those beautiful, fire-colored leggings, listened carefully to Sun's breathing until Sun seemed asleep. Then Coyote crept over to where the leggings hung, took them down, and set off out of the tipi at a run. "Hoh!" he thought, "Now I'll be as great a hunter as Sun, and I'll never be hungry again — no more eating ants!"

Coyote ran for what seemed a long time, then sat down to rest for a moment. But he fell asleep, and slept right through until he heard Sun's great voice saying, "Hoh! You Coyote! What are you doing with my leggings?"

Coyote opened his eyes and saw that he was still in Sun's tipi with the delicate colors of the sunrise everywhere, and if he'd had time to think he would have had to admit it was beautiful. But Sun was standing over him and the leggings were right there in Coyote's hand. "Oh, my friend," Coyote said, "I took them down to look at and I admired them so long I must have fallen asleep. They are such a wonderfully decorated pair of leggings."

Sun didn't say anything to that, but put the leggings back

in their place on the tipi wall. Then it was time for Sun to take his walk across the world. Coyote came out with Sun into the middle of the sunrise there in the east and noted again how bright his own fur had become. Coyote thought the gentler glow of sunrise would be nicer to live with than the more vivid colors of sunset, though he had to admit the variety would be nice, too.

"My friend," said Sun, who seemed to have been fooled by Coyote's story about falling asleep with the leggings in his hand, "make yourself at home. There's food in the bags back there in the tipi, and sweet water in the large gourd. But stay in the tipi during the middle of the day, or you'll still be here in the east when I eat supper in the west."

Coyote spent a peaceful enough morning wandering in the east, coming back to the tipi every now and then for food. Toward the middle of the day Coyote went inside and spent a while trying to see clearly whatever part of the tipi wall was in front of him, but he couldn't. So instead he took Sun's leggings down from the wall and admired their stitching until he thought the middle of the day had passed. After a while he went outside, into the west of the world, and prowled around. He noticed several patches of burned brush scattered here and there away from the tipi.

That evening Sun didn't bother to hunt; they'd have deer meat for several days, even with Coyote's appetite. And that night Coyote took the leggings again after Sun was asleep. This time he decided to run all night and hide when it was almost time for sunrise. So he ran on and on, long after he thought he was surely too tired to run any longer, and when it was almost morning he hid himself in a clump of brush and lay down to sleep.

He'd hardly closed his eyes when Sun's great voice woke him. "Hoh! Coyote! You've got the leggings again!"

Coyote opened his eyes and saw he was still in Sun's tipi, with the leggings tucked under his head this time. "Oh, my friend," he said, "you sleep well on this hard ground, but it hurts my head, and so I got myself something for a pillow during the night. In the dark I didn't know it was your beautiful leggings. They're much too nice to make a pillow of." Sun said nothing, but put the leggings back on the wall.

Coyote tried again on the third night, this time hiding under some rocks when morning came close, and again sunrise found him still in Sun's tipi. The fourth night Coyote decided to just keep running into daylight, thinking that maybe something happened while he slept to bring him back, but when it got light he found himself running as fast as he could right in the center of Sun's tipi.

This time Sun didn't take the leggings back, but said, "Coyote, I don't think you'll have any peace until I give you those leggings. Next time you think about taking something out of Sun's tipi, remember this story, and that you're always in Sun's tipi, which is the world. Now take your leggings and run along." Then Coyote couldn't see the tipi anymore but found himself out on the prairie carrying his new leggings.

"Well," Coyote said, "see what I've gotten this time through my cleverness," and he walked along, looking for brush that might hide deer, or even a rabbit. "And then maybe I will do something," Coyote said to himself, since no one else was around to hear. After running all night he was terribly hungry, and Sun hadn't given him any breakfast.

Soon Coyote came to a little clump of brush. He was too impatient to wait, so he put on the leggings and began to dance. As Coyote circled the brush for the fourth time, he had his bow out and an arrow ready. The brush burst into flame and a rabbit ran out, right at Coyote.

Only Coyote didn't shoot at the rabbit, because the leggings had burst into flame along with the brush, and he was busy trying to slap the fire out. That didn't work but burnt his paws instead, so he lay down and rolled, trying to smother the fire. That didn't work either; instead it set the grass on fire. Then Coyote took off running for a river he remembered nearby, setting a whole long strip of prairie on fire as he ran, driving game of all sorts before him. If he had stopped to hunt he could have supplied himself with meat for a whole winter. But the flames were burning him, and Coyote kept running.

Finally he reached the river and jumped in and the flames went out — not even flames from Sun's own leggings could burn up a river. But the leggings were ruined, and the fur on

Coyote's hind legs was burnt off short. His front paws were burned too, from trying to slap the fire out, and his fur was all spotted and streaked from the sparks and ashes, the way it still is today.

For a while Coyote lay in the shallows crying and feeling sorry for himself. Then he heard Sun overhead, laughing at him for trying to steal those leggings. Since then Coyote hasn't liked Sun so well as he likes Moon. That's why Coyote never sings to the sun, but likes to sing to the moon.

Coyote Learns a Lesson

After his visit to Sun, Coyote decided he should see more of this new world, and from time to time he would travel around. But there was a problem when he traveled away from home; he'd get hungry and have to look for food, and sometimes his appetite was so large it got him in trouble.

On one of his trips, Coyote was walking in the hills along a large river when he came across a herd of deer. Because it was still very early in the world's story, these were the only deer in the world. Coyote didn't know that, but he did know they were deer, because he'd watched all the animals come up out of the cave, back when the ground was still wet; and from his visit to Sun he knew their meat was good to eat. Being Coyote, he thought he was hungry enough to eat them all. But Coyote isn't as large and strong as Wolf, and even Wolf can't hunt a whole herd of deer at once, so Coyote knew he'd have to be clever if he was going to have the feast he dreamed of.

"Hello, friends," Coyote said. In those days, all animals could speak both their own language and another language that all animals understood and people could understand, too. (Some say animals can still speak, but they're too angry at the

way humans treat them to ever speak that language where
humans might hear it.) Coyote spoke in the deer language so
these deer would think he was a friend and know he wasn't
just any ordinary coyote, either, but *the* Coyote.

"Hello, Grandfather Coyote," the deer said. This was a lot
more polite than what some people might have said, which
would have been, "Hello, Old Man Coyote," except in the
Southwest where they might have said, "Hello, Coyote Old
Man." Since Coyote never gets any older, it always puzzles
him that people call him Grandfather. But they do it because
he's *the* Coyote, the same way they call *the* Grizzly Bear,
Grandfather Bear, and *the* Deer, Grandfather Deer — mean-
ing the first one, the one that's both him- or herself and the
spirit of all deer, bear, or coyotes.

And of course Coyote isn't only the spirit of all coyotes,
but he's maybe the most powerful being that walks on the
earth — only most of the time he can't remember that. If
Coyote could remember how much power he has — power to
change shape, power to change things around him, power to
say how things will be — he would really be dangerous since
he's not very responsible. When Coyote does a good thing, it's
usually an accident. And this day, he wasn't out to do any
good things.

But he also wasn't sure how to go about turning all these
deer into one huge Coyote feast. So, since food was on his
mind, he said, "Do you have enough to eat, my friends?" Well,

the deer said, not as much as they'd like, because it was very early in the springtime, and the grass wasn't really coming up very thick yet.

Hmmm, Coyote said. He'd noticed that, too. It almost looked like the deer had forgotten to dance that year. Now that puzzled the deer; they hadn't heard anything about dancing. Coyote, as usual, was making the world up as he went along, and at this time, no one knew about dancing.

Coyote pretended to be very surprised, and wondered — out loud, of course — if the deer really didn't know that a dance to Grandmother Grass would give her strength in the spring, and also let her know how much the deer appreciated her coming up each year, so she would keep coming back? Earth-the-Mother would also be pleased by the touch of their feet as they danced, which feels differently to her than just walking or running.

What Coyote said sounded true to the deer, but they didn't know any dances. Well, Coyote said, he'd teach them. So he showed them the steps, staying on all fours in his coyote shape, though something about the dances didn't feel quite right when he did them on four legs. The deer copied his steps, and soon they were moving around him in a circle, a little awkwardly for deer, while Coyote tried to figure out how to make this dancing work for him.

Then he got an idea, and told the deer to practice while he took some cloth out of the little pack he carries and tore it into strips. Then Coyote told the deer they'd practiced enough, and he had one more thing to say. "Now, my friends, there is another part to this dance. You know that Grandmother Grass lies in the earth, in the dark, and then comes up into the light; and so you must each wear one of these strips of cloth over your eyes, and when I tell you, remove the cloth, but slowly, as though you are Grandmother Grass coming up out of the earth."

With that, Coyote tied a blindfold across each deer's eyes and started them dancing again. This time, he kept them moving in a straight line, right up to the edge of a nearby bluff. He stood at the edge and called, "Come this way, come this way, it's almost time to remove your blindfolds, come this way," as each deer danced past him and over the bluff. Coyote knew, of course, that such a fall would kill all the deer, and then he'd feast on deer meat.

Finally, only one deer was left, a young female, pregnant with twins, who hadn't been able to keep up. Coyote had been so busy fooling the others and dreaming of deer meat that he hadn't noticed how far behind she'd gotten. Finally, the young mother deer had to slip the blindfold up just a little to see where the other deer were, and couldn't get it back down completely with her hooves. As she danced up to Coyote and the few remaining deer at the edge of the cliff, she saw that he was leading the others to dance off the edge. When she danced closer and finally all the way up to the edge, the young mother saw the other deer lying dead on the ground far below and knew what Coyote was doing. Yet, with Coyote singing the Grass Dance song and telling her to dance forward, she couldn't stop herself.

"Coyote!" she cried out. "Coyote! You know it is early in this story! If you let me dance off this bluff with my babies unborn, there won't be any more deer in the whole long story of the world!" And as she said it she was weeping for the deer lying dead at the bottom of the cliff, and for the unborn fawns in her womb, and for herself as well.

No deer? thought Coyote. No deer? No delicious venison? No warm buckskin clothing? He didn't want that, even as hungry as he was. "You are right, my little sister. Dance in that direction," and he pointed away from the cliff's edge, "so that there will be deer in the world." He sang until the young mother deer was out of sight. And so there are still deer in the world.

Now all that dancing had pleased Earth-the-Mother, just as Coyote had said it would. She had leaned close to listen, puzzled because something about the dancing seemed a little odd, even though this was the first time anyone had danced in the young story of the world. The singing sounded odd, too, more like a coyote's howl than real singing.

When she saw what Coyote was doing, Earth-the-Mother became angry. The young deer mother was speaking as Earth-the-Mother leaned close. Earth-the-Mother held her anger for a moment to listen, held her anger as the young deer danced away, and held her anger as Coyote turned to look over the bluff at his waiting feast. Then, as Coyote trotted along the bluff's edge looking for an easy way down, Earth-the-Mother let her anger have its way.

Earth-the-Mother began tearing up her own body to get at Coyote: the land before him opened up, or dropped away entirely; trees sailed by his head, still in the ground where they had always grown; hills stood up to fall on him. A river changed its course and followed Coyote, and he ran, and dodged, and ran again, and couldn't get away from the river. The hills rose up to hem him in, and he scrabbled up their steep sides until they opened to drop him into a ravine, and here came the river, still pursuing.

Earth-the-Mother kept Coyote running for days without sleep. Sometimes she stopped for a while to fool him, and when he began to sleep, the earth moved again. Earth-the-Mother threw mountains at Coyote, then dropped them into a valley, trying to get Coyote down at the bottom with the mountain on top of him. More than once Coyote thought she had him, down at the bottom with the earth closing over his head, but he got out somehow. Sometimes he seemed to have changed into a bird and flown out, then changed back into Coyote to avoid the trees and boulders Earth-the-Mother sent flying through the air. Once it seemed to him that he became very small, like an ant, and crawled out of a tight place.

Finally Coyote was squealing and begging, promising to be good and never kill Earth-the-Mother's children except out of need for food or clothing, and she relented and stopped tearing up her body. The earth grew calm again, and after he had recovered from his fright Coyote said everyone should listen and he would tell them how things should be: that no one should kill except out of need for food or clothing, and never kill more than was needed. To help everyone remember, Coyote said they should speak to the spirit of the being whose body they had need of and explain their need — which has been the right way of things ever since, in this whole long story of the world. When people hunt deer, they speak first to Grandfather Deer, the deer-spirit, to explain their need, and when they cut down oak trees they speak first to Grandfather Oak to explain that need.

What Coyote had told the deer about the Grass Dance was also true. Only it wasn't the deer who should do the Grass Dance, it was people, and people hadn't entered into the story yet. So Coyote turned out to be right about the dancing, even if he didn't get it exactly right the first time.

Coyote's Carving

Sometime after that, Wolf stopped by for another visit. He and Coyote sat around, not doing much of anything. Coyote was carving on a stick he'd found, when Wolf spoke up and said there ought to be people in the world. Coyote didn't know what people were, but that didn't hinder his boasting. He claimed he'd already begun carving some.

Wolf looked over Coyote's shoulder at the straight branch Coyote had been whittling, and laughed. "People ought to have arms and legs, they shouldn't be straight up and down like a stake." Coyote said he was just adding those. Then Wolf pointed out that people ought to have heads, too, and Coyote was just carving a head now. Wolf said one person wasn't enough, there ought to be more, and Coyote was just going for more sticks. He carved twenty like the first one — now that he knew what people ought to look like — and spread them out on the ground, proud of what he'd done.

Wolf laughed some more and said people ought to be able to move around, and Coyote said he was just coming to that. He took the stick figures and threw them into a hole he'd dug out of an anthill the week before to see if the ants had anything good down there, and told the sticks to lie down for a while, then become people. Coyote was tired of the whole thing. He figured Wolf would forget about the sticks down in the anthole and quit bothering him about them.

The next day Coyote had forgotten the sticks and planned to go hunting; but Wolf hadn't forgotten, and made him come along to look even though Coyote said he was busy and didn't really have the time. When they looked in the anthole the stick figures were just lying there. Wolf started to laugh again, but Coyote said, "No, that's good, that's what I wanted. They're stubborn and don't want to admit they're people, but after the ants bite them a while they'll get up. They're alive now, they're just trying to help you fool me by pretending not to be." He said that to quiet Wolf, who was still laughing because Coyote's people hadn't come to life. Then Coyote and Wolf went someplace else for a while.

The second day Coyote again wanted to go hunting, but Wolf said, "Let's go look in the hole first." So they came back. The stick figures were still lying on the ground, but they were quivering a little when the ants bit, and some of the bites were turning dull pink in the pale wood.

"Well," Coyote said, "you see, they're learning not to fool me. We'll look again tomorrow." Wolf wasn't laughing quite so hard this time, though he wondered if the sticks were really quivering, or if the ants were moving them around.

The third day both Wolf and Coyote wanted to go look.

This time there wasn't any doubt: the sticks were bouncing around down in the anthole and turning bright red from all the bites. Coyote nodded sagely as though this were just what he'd expected, and said they'd come back the next day. As they were leaving, Wolf thought he heard a kind of whimper from down in the anthole, but he didn't say anything.

On the fourth day it was Wolf who wanted to go hunting, but Coyote said, "No, first let's go look at those people I made." So they went and looked into the anthole. This time they saw some fine, tall, strong people with black hair and eyes, looking up at them and dancing as they slapped at the ants, which were biting them unmercifully. "You up there," they called. "Help us get out of this hole and away from these ants! They're eating us alive!"

Coyote looked over at Wolf and laughed. "You see how my magic works? They admit they're alive now!" He leaned back over to look at the people. "You in the hole! If I let you out, do you promise to stay alive and to live on this earth and be people, and do the dances when they should be done?"

The people in the hole thought that was a strange thing to ask, since they were already people, and they thought Coyote should be able to see that they were already dancing. No one had told them this story yet and they couldn't remember being carved sticks that Coyote threw into an anthole, so they said, "Certainly we'll remain alive and do the dances if you let us out of this hole. If you don't let us out soon, these ants will eat us completely and we won't be anywhere." Coyote said that might be a good thing, too, but he'd let them out of the hole anyway, and he turned around and hung his tail over the edge for them to grab onto.

The people all grabbed hold and began trying to climb out at once. Coyote, who'd forgotten that it hurts to have even one person pull your tail, was so startled that he jumped and pulled them all out of the hole. He turned around and looked at all the people he'd pulled up, laughed again, and said to Wolf, "See, I pull them all out at once because I'm so strong. Your tail probably couldn't take that." Then he looked again and saw that some of the people were women and said, "What's this? I don't remember carving them. How did they get into this story?"

Wolf pointed out that his people were all red from the antbites, and Coyote said yes, that was part of his plan so you could tell they weren't wood anymore. He told the people to go lie in the mud by the river until the antbites were better, and he showed them where the river was and what mud was. Even after the antbites healed, the people didn't fade but remained a beautiful deep coppery red color.

Coyote said, "See, that's how you make people," though he was still trying to figure out how some of them got to be women, and how they all became so much taller than he was. Wolf eventually figured it out, but Wolf was still mad about that remark about hanging around the edge of the buffalo herd, so he wouldn't tell.

Coyote still doesn't know that it was all because the anthill was in the earth. Earth-the-Mother liked the people's dancing, even if at first they danced only because of the ants, so she gave the people size, strength, and beauty. And, of course, Earth-the-Mother made sure some of them were women so there would be mothers, and people could go on and do the ceremonial dances when it was time. Coyote didn't really create women; and ever since, women have teased men for being created by a crackbrain like Coyote.

Coyote and the Crow
Buffalo-Ranchers

Those people Coyote carved liked it that there were both women and men. They liked it so much that soon new people were everywhere, and they were busy at all kinds of things. Some of those things weren't very good, but people had scattered out so widely that a few got away with mischief for a long time before anyone noticed.

Way off from where Coyote lived was a small village, and in it there was a family who trapped all the buffalo and hid them in a hole in the ground. They set their tipi over the mouth of that hole so they could watch over it, and made people give them things in exchange for buffalo meat. They could do this because their men were fierce, strong warriors, and no one could stand against them. Soon they had almost all the goods in the village while the other people were starving and weeping.

During this time Wolf had gotten tired of watching Coyote do things and had gone off somewhere again, so Coyote came walking alone to that village. He was hungry, as usual, and looking for a handout, but the people only wept louder when he begged for food. At first Coyote thought his hard-luck story had been so good it was causing their sorrow, and he smiled all over inside at the thought of the meal they'd give him when they were able to control themselves again.

When two days passed and no food appeared, Coyote was hungrier than ever. Finally he asked someone what was the matter. It was an old woman he asked, one who was too starved and hungry even to weep any longer, and she told him about the family who had captured all the buffalo.

Coyote grew angry then, and he puffed himself up and stomped all over the village talking about what he would do, until he passed by the tipi where the buffalo were hidden and saw how big were the warriors who lived there. Then he became quiet, and finally he approached the old woman again.

"Grandmother," he said to her, "I will help you, and maybe I will help everyone else. I will be a wooden dish, a lovely carved wooden dish, and you will take me to those people and trade me for meat. When they take me inside their tipi, maybe I will do something."

The old woman who was too weak even to cry stirred herself then and took the dish which Coyote had become. She supposed Coyote could change his shape when he wasn't scared, even if no stories before then said he could — probably he'd just thought of it for the first time. She took the dish to the buffalo-ranchers and offered it to them for some meat. She drove a hard bargain and got an entire hind quarter for it, enough to make stew for everyone. Soon all the people in the village were huddling in their tipis, eating stew, and waiting to see what Coyote would do.

The family of buffalo-ranchers took the Coyote-dish into their tipi and used it to hold the roast meat for their meal that night. Somehow the meat was eaten more rapidly that evening than usual, though everyone claimed not to have had a second helping. The women scolded everyone, saying there was no reason to lie about how much they'd eaten, since they had all the buffalo in the world down in the hole behind the fire.

Still no one would admit to eating more than his share, and the buffalo-ranchers became angry, quarreled, and went to bed unhappy with one another. Someone noticed the dish quivering once, but thought it was because of the way they were all shouting and stomping as they argued.

The quivering was, of course, Coyote laughing at his own joke. He was so pleased, in fact, that he almost turned back into himself so he could leap up and run away into the night, shouting, "Hoh! I fooled you! Your dish is Coyote, and I've been eating the meat!" The women mentioned the hole with the buffalo in it just in time to remind Coyote of his real reason for being a dish.

After the people were asleep, Coyote-the-dish managed to slide over to where they'd set a rock over the hole behind the fire. Then he changed himself into an ant and crept past the rock into the hole. There, indeed, were all the buffalo in the young world, standing as far as even Coyote's eyes could see. They weren't happy, either, about living in a hole instead of running free on the prairies.

Coyote told them to get ready, and when he lifted the rock

off to run as fast as they could out of the tipi and away, and never let themselves be captured like that again. Then he crept back out, turned himself into Coyote, picked up the rock — it was a big rock — and threw it through the tipi entrance, tearing a doorway large enough for buffalo.

The buffalo came boiling up out of the ground, one after the other after the other, and ran out through the entrance, past the other tipis, and into the night. The people living in the other tipis had all stayed inside, because with Coyote around trying to do something you didn't know what might happen. That was a good thing, because buffalo came out all night long, and someone probably would have been trampled. A few old grandmothers and brave warriors looked out, and said it was a thing to see when the buffalo-ranchers' tipi started erupting buffalo.

Of course, when the buffalo started running through their home, the buffalo-ranchers woke up and all their warriors reached for weapons and said hard things to Coyote, who was still standing by the hole, enjoying himself. When he saw the weapons he got scared, and before he thought, he said, "I wish you were crows! Crows! Crows, I said, I wish you were crows — and stuck in the smokehole!"

All the people in the tent drifted upwards to the smokehole and became very small, with beaks, wings, and claws, and white — because crows were white then. Coyote looked up, not understanding what he'd done for a moment, and then was as pleased as though he'd meant to do it. "Yes," he said to himself, because the buffalo weren't listening, they were just running, "that is a good thing. And maybe I will do something else, too."

When the buffalo had all run out of the hole, Coyote went to the entrance and called to the people to bring him wood, and he built a fire using the greenest pieces. He smoked the buffalo-rancher crows for four days, until they were as black as they could be. Before he let them go, Coyote told them to remember their lesson: he said from now on they should hunt when they were hungry, just like everyone else.

Then he told the people in the village to come and take back the things they'd traded to the buffalo-ranchers, and to fix him some buffalo meat. Some of the buffalo had hurt themselves running out of the hole, and the people had been able to kill them the next morning right there in camp, so there was enough for everyone, even Coyote.

It was a long time before anybody tried to start another buffalo-ranch. The crow buffalo-ranchers still hang around where people live, though, trying to steal food, whether from people's gardens and fields or from their drying racks. Crows have never liked Coyote since then. They'll follow him for miles across the prairie, cawing and cawing — insults in crow-talk. Coyote kind of likes it. Though he can't always remember what the crows are angry about, he knows they wouldn't insult him so if he hadn't done something powerful.

Coyote's Eyes

❖　❖　❖

One day Coyote was out walking across the prairie. Some crows had been following him for most of the day, cawing insults, and had just gotten tired and flown away to the north where Coyote had been coming from. Coyote hardly had time to enjoy the quiet when he heard something just over the next rise to the south. Being Coyote, he thought he'd sneak up and see what it was, just in case it might be something good to eat. While Coyote wasn't hungry just then, he thought he might get hungry later and it would be too bad if he passed up something good. So he slunk up the little rise of land, and when he got close to the top he dropped down on his belly and wriggled the rest of the way up to some sagebrush. Only his eyes and ears and his sharp nose were showing.

Just a little way away — about three Coyote bounds, he thought — a little bird sat on a dead log, chirping happily at the world. Coyote flattened himself even further, because the bird was looking right at him and he thought sure he'd been seen. But the bird just kept on chirping and so Coyote unflattened enough to get a second look, then rose up a little further, not worrying any longer about being seen because the little bird had no eyes. It had places where eyes should have been, all right, but no eyes in those places.

That puzzled Coyote. What was this bird so happy about, if it had no eyes? How did it keep from starving to death? And how did it avoid its enemies? It was like Coyote to think of starving to death first, and of enemies only later. Coyote, of course, would have said that was because there was no one brave enough to be his enemy, but Wolf would have said it was because Coyote was always hungry.

Coyote decided to stay right where he was, tucked snug in the shadow of the sagebrush where even Sun wouldn't be able to see him, and watch the bird. It must have some great power to sit there chirping so calmly with possible enemies all around, Coyote thought.

Coyote didn't think the bird was a very handsome fellow: a sort of nondescript gray and brown, with a little yellow on its breast, but not enough yellow to look so proud about. Its song wasn't much, either, just a whole lot of chirps. Just then the bird trilled a long and lovely liquid sound, and sat up a little straighter, leaning forward almost as though it *could* see something coming out of the south.

Coyote scrunched farther under the sagebrush and peeked out very cautiously. He had to look very hard, but finally Coyote saw two dots flying toward him, up there in the sky. At first he thought they were birds a long way off, maybe friends who took care of the blind bird. Then he realized that those dots were pretty close, no more than a bowshot away, and they really *were* round dots with no wings. They were half the size of the tip of one of Coyote's little fingers if he'd had his hands on just then, which he didn't because paws were better for sneaking up on blind birds.

Finally Coyote realized that the two flying dots were eyes, tiny bird eyes, yellowish gray, and making right for the bird. Coyote went absolutely flat under the sagebrush where they couldn't see him, only raising his head a little bit so he could see.

Sure enough, the eyes flew right to the bird and floated gently back where they belonged. But even though the bird now had eyes, it didn't look around very carefully, and Coyote was able to keep one of his own sharp eyes where he could see what the bird would do next.

The bird sat for a while, glancing around at things, and then turned to face west. The bird had been facing south, the direction from which the eyes had come; Coyote had come from the north, so the flying eyes hadn't seen him on their way out, and he'd kept pretty low as they came back. The bird said, "Eyes, I want to see. Eyes, I want to see," and its eyes left its face again and flew off, to the west this time.

Hoh! thought Coyote, that's a pretty good trick! Let's see how he does it. And he waited and watched, and after a while the eyes came back again, and reentered the bird's head. Then the bird turned north and sent the eyes out again, while Coyote

lay flat under the sagebrush and hoped they wouldn't see him
this time either. Now, Coyote knew that powerful things often
come in fours, and that anyone doing things in a ritual manner
begins in the east and ends in the north, so he figured this
would be the last time the bird sent those eyes out. As soon
as the eyes had gone and the bird was blind again, Coyote
made three Coyote leaps and seized the bird in his front paws,
which he then changed to hands because it's easier to hold
things with hands.

The little bird was too terrified even to chirp, which gave
Coyote time to catch his breath, say who he was, and demand
that the bird teach him the trick. Otherwise, Coyote said, he'd
eat the bird for lunch now, and its eyes for dessert when they
returned. And so of course the bird showed him how to do
the trick, how to face each direction in turn and say, "Eyes, I
want to see. Eyes, I want to see." But, the bird warned, the
trick could be done only four times a day; any more would
bring bad luck.

Coyote eagerly agreed to everything the bird said, learned
the trick, and wandered off, happy. He could see all sorts of
possibilities for a trick like this one. He wouldn't have to go
look for food, but would just send his eyes; he wouldn't have
to look for mischief, either. And once he'd found some mischief, he wouldn't have to keep looking over his shoulder to
see if anyone was coming. Instead he'd just send his eyes out
to make sure no one was watching, and then get into the

mischief after his eyes had told him it was safe. Already he was forgetting what the bird had told him about doing the trick four times and facing each direction.

After a while, Coyote started wondering if the trick would really work, if the bird had told him everything. Maybe there was a magic stone or something the bird had kept hidden, and the trick wouldn't work now that he wasn't near the bird. He said, "Maybe I should do something just now," and sat down and said, "Eyes, I want to see. Eyes, I want to see." Sure enough, his eyes left their sockets and floated up and away. He happened to be facing south, not east, so that was the way his eyes went. After a while they returned, and Coyote saw everything they had seen: mostly empty prairie, but here and there a jackrabbit or a meadowlark, and off a ways, antelope tracks, going east. Ah, Coyote thought, what a wonderful trick.

Coyote wandered on, heading west, and after a while he tried the trick again, looking ahead to see if there was anything interesting. Then he tried the trick again, and again — that made four times. He'd sent the eyes out twice to the west, once to the south, and once to the north, and not to the east at all. But Coyote had lost count, or had forgotten what the bird had said, or maybe (because he was Coyote) he just didn't care, and he sat down a fifth time and said, "Eyes, I want to see. Eyes, I want to see." This time his eyes floated up and away and did not come back.

Coyote sat crying and reproaching himself for a while. Then

he began to stumble along, bumping into things and falling over them, blind as if he were still a little naked Coyote pup before its eyes were open — though that didn't sound right to Coyote, because he didn't think he'd ever been a little naked pup. He couldn't remember exactly how he'd gotten into the world. Probably, he thought, he'd just walked up one day and said hello to Wolf, and ever since he'd been around, though that didn't sound exactly right, either. For a moment he was almost certain that he'd floated up on a raft, but that didn't make any sense at all to Coyote — what would he be doing on a raft?

Finally, when he'd gotten so hungry he thought he was starving to death, he caught a mouse — quite by accident. He had tripped and fallen into a clump of grass where the mouse was hiding, trapping it under his hollow belly and grabbing quickly before the mouse could gather its wits and escape. Again he changed his paws into hands, so he could feel what he'd caught and tell what it was, which let the mouse know that this wasn't just any coyote but *the* Coyote, even if he was blind.

"Mouse," Coyote said, "I'll let you go if you'll give me one of your wonderfully sharp eyes." The mouse noticed that its eyes suddenly saw much more clearly than they had; it could see every hair on Coyote's sharp muzzle, and could see his long, sharp teeth even more clearly. Still it didn't want to give up one of its new sharp eyes, until Coyote said he was so hungry he might as well eat right now, and fresh mouse was

all he had. Then the mouse gave Coyote an eye, but not its best one.

Coyote put the eye in his socket and he could see, all right, but only a little because the eye was far too small and it rolled around a good deal. The eye saw as though it still belonged to the mouse, so the world looked very large to Coyote. In fact, the mouse looked as big as he was, and he was a little afraid of it, since he'd never seen a mouse that large before and he wasn't sure what it might be able to do to him. So Coyote became very polite as he asked the mouse for one more favor before he let it go: Where was some food?

The mouse led Coyote to some wild raspberries — all berries were wild then — which looked as large as Coyote's own head. Coyote thought just one of those would make a very fine meal. Somehow the berries didn't seem so filling when he got them to his mouth, however, and he had to eat just as many as he would if he'd seen them with his own eyes.

The mouse didn't stay around after Coyote let it go, so Coyote ate alone and didn't have anyone to remind him that the world wasn't really as large as the mouse's eye made it look. He was afraid of everything: a robin flew by, and Coyote actually crawled under the berry bushes in fear of the huge bird his mouse's eye reported. But finally Coyote had enough to eat, and he set out, going west, the direction he'd sent his eyes, hoping to catch up to them.

Every now and then Coyote's eye would roll around in his

head, and he'd find himself looking at the inside of his own skull. It was pretty empty in there, and enough light came in through his ears and the vacant eye socket to let him see that somebody had been writing insults on the back of the inside of his head. The insults were in picture writing, because regular writing hadn't been invented yet.

Coyote had bigger problems to worry about. Sometimes the eye would roll around and fall out and he'd find himself looking at a blade of grass, maybe, or a rock, down on the ground, because he continued to see through the eye until it got further away. Those times he would have to feel around on the ground until he found the eye again, dust it off, and put it back in his head.

Once the eye landed so that it looked up into the sky. When Coyote bent to look for it, he found himself looking up into his own eyeless face, which seemed as large as it would have to the mouse. For a moment he didn't recognize himself and almost ran away.

Coyote wandered on for a while, afraid of everything he met, until he came to a herd of buffalo. Of course Coyote thought these were the biggest buffalo he'd ever seen, but his situation was pretty desperate. He looked them over as carefully as he could through his one rolling eye and finally he picked out an old bull who didn't look as fearsome as the younger bulls.

Coyote walked up to the old bull, begging at the top of his

voice as soon as he was close enough for a bull that old, and maybe a little deaf, to hear him. "Oh, older brother, won't you help me? Look, I've lost both my eyes and have only this mouse's eye and it makes everything too large and you are old and have two eyes and surely you could spare me one since you won't need your eyes much longer and everyone knows that one buffalo eye is as good as two of most eyes."

Now Coyote intended this just as a bit of flattery, because even the buffalo know that buffalo can't see very well; but the old bull noticed immediately that the vision out of his right eye had become much better. The left eye, which was milky and blurred with age, hadn't improved any, however. The old buffalo soon became tired of listening to Coyote's voice, and remembered that Coyote had said he wouldn't need his eyes too much longer anyway, and he knew things Coyote said tended to come true. Maybe, the old bull thought, he could help the other buffalo keep this new sharp vision, so finally he agreed to give Coyote his left eye.

Coyote seized the eye and put it into his other eye socket and walked away, pleased with his own cleverness and his two new eyes. No one, he thought, had such an interesting pair of eyes as he did. But of course the buffalo's eye was too big and would hardly fit, and from time to time it, too, would fall out, and even when it was in it didn't see very well. In fact, this eye saw even worse than the mouse's; it was old, and milky, and everything looked gray and dim through it. That made

Coyote angry. "That old buffalo lied to me," he said. "Buffalo don't see well at all!" And back at the herd the old bull's sight returned to normal. Ah well, the old bull thought, that eye wasn't much good anyway. At least I got rid of Coyote.

The buffalo's eye continued to see as though it were still in the buffalo's head, and so Coyote had one eye that made things look very clear and sharp but too large and one that made them blurry but too small, and he was always confused. Coyote had to choose which eye to believe, and he usually chose wrong. The mouse's eye would tell him that a log in his path was an unclimbable wall, while the buffalo's eye would tell him it was a mere stick; he would believe the buffalo's eye and not step high enough over the log, trip himself, and fall down. Or he would come to a small puddle, and the buffalo's eye would say it was a mere drop, while the mouse's eye would say it was a lake. Coyote would believe the mouse's eye and spend half a day walking around the lake.

Every now and then one of Coyote's eyes would fall out, but he'd keep seeing through the eye as long as it didn't get too far away. That didn't work very well, either; as the eye tumbled to the ground the half of the world it saw would spin while the other half didn't. Sometimes both eyes would fall out and the world would spin two ways at once, and Coyote would get dizzy. Coyote had a hard time with his new eyes.

Coyote's Revenge

Coyote came walking across the prairie, out to look at the world as well as he could with his one mouse eye and his one buffalo eye, until he came upon a village nestled down along a river. Now this was no ordinary village: not only were the tipis larger than most, but none were old and patched. Coyote figured these people had hunted lots of game to have enough hides for that many new lodges. And, yes, as Coyote came closer, he could see plenty of meat hanging on racks to dry for winter storage.

These people had fields full of crops, too: turnips, onions, carrots, all sorts of root crops they could leave in the ground until it froze, squash — lots of squash vines — corn, and lots of other good food. Now that Coyote thought of it, he'd seen plenty of berry bushes just over the hill, and he could see more bushes growing up and down the river. Yes, this was a prosperous village; it had lots of food and warm robes for the winter. Even its location was a good one, nestled down in the hills out of the wind.

Now, Coyote is always hungry, even when he has his own eyes and can see to hunt, so he was happy at the thought of all that food. Since it was getting along toward late fall, he was even happier at the thought of all those warm robes for the winter. Yes, he thought, he'd do this village the honor not just of feeding him a few meals but might, if they deserved it, stay with them all winter.

Coyote wanted to make a good impression, so he stopped up at the top of the last hill to brush the dust off himself, and even to take his finest clothes out of the little pack he always carried. Then he stood up on his hind legs, looking like a human, and walked into the village, convinced he was the finest thing those people had ever seen. As for his eyes, why, that was just another mark of how different he was from normal beings.

When the first few people he passed stopped and stared, Coyote was pleased at the reaction he was getting. But he didn't stop to talk to anyone in the first circle of tipis he passed, or even the second or third. No, Coyote was on his way to the innermost circle, where the most important people (and probably the ones with the most food and warmest robes) would have their tipis.

The more Coyote saw of this camp the more he approved of it. He liked the round shape, though he knew most Indian camps were round — because most things were round; the circle was the holiest shape of all. He also liked the size. Coyote didn't think he'd ever seen a winter camp this large, which meant not only lots of food, but lots of pretty women, too.

Maybe he'd get married this winter.

By the time Coyote got to the innermost circle where the chief people's tipis would be located, he had quite a following of children, young men and women, full-grown adults, and even old people hobbling along behind. Coyote had slowed to a dignified saunter so that even the old people could keep up; it seemed only fair to let them see how the chief persons would honor him. They were all so happy too, laughing and pointing, while the children ran off to bring others who lived on the opposite side of the camp to see what a great one had come.

Here came a group of young men — obviously important young men, from important families; they were dressed almost as well as Coyote himself. Like everyone else, they were so happy to see Coyote they laughed out loud. The way they all pointed was a little impolite, but Coyote figured that if the food held out and he stayed all winter, he could teach them better manners. With someone like Coyote around, the whole village would surely change for the better.

Coyote walked into the center and turned to look at all the people he'd made so happy by his visit. To be polite, he tried not to look anyone in the eye, but he couldn't help but steal a peek at the face of the handsomest and best-dressed of the young men, the one who must be the son of the chief person.

Now, Coyote expected that young man to behave properly, which would mean the young man wouldn't quite look directly into a visitor's eyes, but just to one side, or just a little down, because looking someone right in the eye isn't very polite. But this young man was looking Coyote right in the eyes, staring even, with his face all twisted up strangely so one eye was wide and the other squinched down small. Then Coyote realized that the young man wasn't laughing with pleasure at the sight of Coyote, he was laughing *at* Coyote, as though Coyote were a fool! When Coyote looked around at the other young men, he realized that all of them were laughing at him and pointing at his best clothes — which might have gotten a little wrinkled being in his pack for so long, and perhaps had a little stain here and there, and maybe a tear or two he should have gotten around to mending, but still looked awfully good — screwing up their faces so one eye looked small and the other large, and laughing!

When Coyote looked hard at the people who had followed him all this way, he realized that they, too, were laughing at him. Even the children were making fun, imitating his eyes and his dignified walk through the village! He turned back to face the laughing young men, looking their leader full in the eye so he'd remember every line of the young man's face. And then Coyote turned and ran from the village, dropping to all fours and changing back into his coyote shape as he heard the laughter swell behind him. The laughter seemed to echo for miles as Coyote ran and ran and ran, up through the hills, going away from the village, until finally he could no longer hear it.

Coyote was angry and thought maybe he'd better do something, and even while running away he came up with a plan for revenge. He knew he'd have to act quickly before he forgot that plan, because his memory wasn't always so good. This seemed to be a new story, so he couldn't just find Wolf and ask him how it went if he forgot his plan halfway through; he'd have to make this one up himself, and try to keep it going right.

Coyote's usually pretty lazy, but this time he went straight to work. He set up in a cave he knew about, then killed a deer, drying most of the meat to eat later, because this might take a while with his eyes not working so well. He tanned the hide and carefully made a beautiful buckskin dress from it. Then he went to Old Lady Porcupine and talked her out of some quills. He really didn't have to talk very much; it was almost as though she knew this story, even though Coyote didn't (and he thought he knew all the Coyote stories, since he was supposed to have been in them). Coyote made some dye and dyed the quills, using them to decorate the dress. But he was a little careless, or maybe his eyes tricked him; anyway, he broke some of the quills, so he had to go back to Porcupine to ask for more.

This time Old Lady Porcupine said no, he should have been more careful. (How'd she know that? Coyote wondered. Maybe I should just ask her how this story comes out, since she seems to know it all in advance — but he didn't.) Coyote begged and wheedled, and finally lost his temper and told Porcupine her quills were ugly, that's why he broke some. She got angry and swatted him with her tail so he was speared by lots of her quills. Then Coyote danced away, boasting, "I fooled you, ouch! I — ouch! — fooled you! I got the quills I wanted, I fooled — ouch — you!" He was just as proud of himself as though he'd planned to get all stuck with porcupine quills.

Coyote finished decorating the dress and some moccasins he'd made, too. But he'd need more than just the dress to impress those people in the village, so he went to a place where he knew an old grizzly bear had died. When he got there, he spoke to the Bear Spirit and said, "Grandfather Bear, I have need of your teeth and claws, and even your hide and skull, so I ask you to let me have them and not be angry at me because I've taken them." Then he took the teeth from the bear's skull to make a necklace, its claws to make bracelets, and its hide to make a robe. But before he went off and made those things, he took the bear's skull to a place just below a cliff, climbed the cliff, and dropped a boulder onto the skull below so it was crushed. Then Coyote climbed back down the cliff, picked up the crushed skull, and took it back to the cave.

All that was the easy part. Now Coyote stood up on his hind legs and became a human again. He took hold of the hair on his head and pulled it out long like a woman's, yelping some because pulling on his hair that way hurt. Then he went down to a quiet pond near the cave and used it for a mirror so he could reshape his face into that of a beautiful young woman. When he was done, Coyote looked into the water and saw the face of a young woman so lovely — most of all her eyes, which were a perfect match for each other — he forgot what he was doing and jumped in the water after her, but that only got him wet.

Finally Coyote was ready. He changed completely into a woman and put on the dress and moccasins. With the bear-tooth necklace, the bear-claw bracelets, and the bear skull in his pouch he set off for the village where he'd been treated badly.

The people living on the edge of the village noticed Coyote this time, too, when he came walking with a maiden's small steps, keeping his eyes modestly down. Again they followed him as he walked through the circles toward the camp's center. But this time they were quiet and respectful. The children were kept quiet or told to go away, and a fast-running young man went ahead to the chief person's lodge in the village center. The young men, with the handsomest one at their head, stopped a full ring of tipis away. There they chattered and glanced at Coyote more directly and more often than was polite — but at least they were trying to be polite this time, Coyote thought. They just weren't very good at it.

Coyote kept his eyes lowered — as was polite for any young person, even if the young men in this village didn't seem to know it — and stopped in front of the village's finest lodge. There the chief person, a tall woman no longer so young but not so old either, stepped forward to greet him. Coyote kept his eyes lowered until Woman-Chief asked, "What is your name, young woman, and what brings you to visit us here?"

Coyote hadn't thought about a name, and in his confusion could only stammer, "I — I am not Coyote!"

"Not-Coyote," said Woman-Chief. "It is an unusual name, and, I think, a powerful one. Will you come inside my lodge and take something to eat and drink?"

Now there's nothing Coyote likes better than to eat and drink, but since Coyote had spoken the words saying he was not Coyote, he could no longer be Coyote, with all of Coyote's cunning and guile. Instead, she was a confused young woman named Not-Coyote who didn't know anything about herself except what Coyote had planned for her to be. Not-Coyote did seem to be hungry after her journey, so she eagerly followed Woman-Chief into the tipi.

As they sat eating and drinking, Not-Coyote told Woman-Chief what she could remember of the life Coyote had made up for her: that, indeed, she was not married; that she lived up in the hills with her father and four strong brothers; and that, hearing of Woman-Chief's village, her father had sent Not-Coyote to see whether the village might contain suitable wives for his four strong sons.

Perhaps, Woman-Chief inquired, Not-Coyote might be interested in a husband for herself? Not-Coyote was too bashful to answer such a question, but her blushes and pleased smile were answer enough. Not-Coyote couldn't exactly remember the plan she'd made up when she'd been Coyote, but it had something to do with being married — she could remember that much.

Then Woman-Chief excused herself for a brief time, and when she returned she brought her son, who was of course the same handsome and well-dressed young man who'd led the laughing at Coyote a time ago. Not-Coyote wasn't surprised. She remembered that Coyote had thought that this might be the way this story would go, once it got started.

The young man was most respectful, despite his strange name: Stares-them-in-the-Face. He looked down at Not-Coyote's feet, or off to one side, and when he did look at her face he didn't stare rudely into her eyes as he'd done into Coyote's. He was, Woman-Chief said, single, and Not-Coyote could see by his clothing that he was a good hunter and there would be many robes and much meat in his lodge.

Now, Coyote wouldn't have been so sure of that; he would have suspected that whole bunch of laughing young men were sit-around-the-village people while others did the work. But Not-Coyote was the most innocent young maiden ever, since she'd only been Not-Coyote for a very little while, and was willing enough to believe in a handsome young man like Stares-them-in-the-Face. In fact, Not-Coyote found him very interesting, and not just for his fine clothing, either. Then Woman-Chief said, look at the sewing and the bead work in Stares-them-in-the-Face's clothing; that was her doing, she said, and her fingers were no longer so limber as they had been. The work was nothing so fine as that on Not-Coyote's dress — had Not-Coyote done the work herself?

Well, it was true that Not-Coyote had done the sewing and the bead-work herself, back when she was just Coyote. And she had tanned the deerskin, made the dress and moccasins, and done the fancy quillwork that decorated both. Oh, but she'd almost forgotten, her father and brothers had sent presents for Woman-Chief and her son. Her father had asked her to apologize for not sending more — he and her brothers had been in a hurry to go fight water monsters.

"More than one water monster?" Stares-them-in-the-Face asked, staring.

"Of course," Not-Coyote answered, if there had been just one, her father would have gone alone so her brothers could have come to the village with her. This made Stares-them-in-the-Face stare again. But her father and brothers knew fighting water monsters would take some time and they hadn't wanted Not-Coyote to put off visiting until spring, so they had let her come with just these few gifts.

She wouldn't have had even these poor things, Not-Coyote said, embarrassed, as she took the grizzly bear robe and the necklace and bracelets from her pack, but that just before her father and brothers left, her youngest brother noticed a passing grizzly bear. He had leapt upon it, struck it once on the head with his fist, and asked Not-Coyote to make these gifts from its body as a small token of respect. With that, Not-Coyote gave Woman-Chief the necklace and bracelets, gave the robe to Stares-them-in-the-Face, and last of all showed them the smashed skull from the dead bear's body.

"One blow? Bare-handed? The youngest of your brothers?" gulped Stares-them-in-the-Face, for even to his foolish eyes the skull looked as though a boulder had landed on it.

All this sounded a little odd, even to Not-Coyote, but of course the only things in her mind were what had been placed there back when she'd still been Coyote, and so she was sure these things were true. Woman-Chief wondered a little, too, but she could see the honesty in Not-Coyote's eyes, and believed her. Stares-them-in-the-Face could only see how beautiful Not-Coyote was, and that was enough for him.

Not-Coyote stayed with Woman-Chief for a week, mostly enjoying herself, though she couldn't exactly remember just what her life had been like before she came to Woman-Chief's camp. She spent much of her time with Stares-them-in-the-Face, and now that she was a beautiful woman, she didn't mind his staring so much. In fact, Not-Coyote found him kind of attractive, though his manners did need work.

From time to time Not-Coyote would almost remember that she was really Coyote, and male, and that this was all an elaborate revenge plan to shame Stares-them-in-the-Face and his whole village — which had begun to call itself The-Place-Coyote-Ran-From, for the day they laughed Coyote out of camp. All said they hadn't known it was Coyote until he changed shape, there on the edge of the camp circle, so he could run away faster on all fours. Stares-them-in-the-Face was the hero of that story, which kept growing every time he told it, and kept Not-Coyote from falling too much in love with him. Still, Not-Coyote did have to admit, now that she looked at him with woman's eyes, that Stares-them-in-the-Face was good-looking, in a spoiled sort of way.

At the end of the week, Woman-Chief spoke to her about a marriage with Stares-them-in-the-Face. Not-Coyote confessed that her father had heard of Stares-them-in-the-Face and had hoped a marriage might happen, if she cared for Stares-them-in-the-Face once they'd met; and, she said very softly, she did.

With that, Woman-Chief stood, walked outside into the very center of the village, and called her people together. She called four times, though once would have been enough. Woman-Chief had led this village for a long time, and she had led it well: her people would listen to what she said.

When the people had gathered, Woman-Chief raised her voice and said, "Not-Coyote comes from a truly illustrious family, and will do our village great honor by marrying my son, Stares-them-in-the-Face! The wedding will be held tomorrow! Prepare for the celebration!" Not-Coyote kept her eyes modestly on the ground, as was fitting for a maiden, and even Stares-them-in-the-Face looked down, though just for a moment before he was looking boldly at Not-Coyote again.

Now Coyote's original plan had been to wait until the wedding ceremony was almost over, and then reveal who he really was so he could laugh as loudly as he knew how at Stares-them-in-the-Face for almost marrying Coyote, and at the villagers for being fooled, too. But when he'd made that plan, he'd been Coyote; now he was Not-Coyote, an innocent young girl who'd never seen any young men but her brothers before. Stares-them-in-the-Face, for all his rudeness and laziness, was tall and handsome, and so obviously in love with Not-Coyote that, yes, she was a little flattered by that, too. Then the preparations had taken so long, and it was now late in the fall, snow would come any day, and this camp had lots of food and plenty of robes. Well, it would certainly be a warm place to spend the winter, as Coyote had thought back when he'd first come into the village.

So with all these things going through her head, and because it was so hard to remember that she was really Coyote, Not-Coyote somehow didn't laugh or change back into Coyote and run away near the end of the wedding ceremony. Spring, she told herself, would be a better time for that. Even if she had remembered who she really was and just why Coyote had made this plan, she might have decided that she could reveal herself in spring, after a comfortable winter, and shame Stares-them-in-the-Face then, as well as she could have now.

By spring, Not-Coyote had completely forgotten why she'd wanted to shame that village. And while Stares-them-in-the-Face wasn't a perfect husband — he was lazy, as Coyote had thought, and though they had plenty, it was mostly because the village gave them food and robes out of respect for Woman-Chief — he was still handsome and, well, she might even be in love with him, a little. Then, too, Not-Coyote was expecting a child; that was clear by late spring, when it would have been a good time to reveal herself and laugh and run away. Not-Coyote wasn't even sure she could change back into Coyote, pregnant as she was, so she decided to stay a while longer. Besides, this way the child would have a good home when it came time to leave.

But of course the child wasn't born until fall, when winter wasn't so far off, and Not-Coyote decided to stay until spring — and by spring she was carrying another child. Now, she had almost forgotten what she was doing in the village. By the third spring she'd spent in that village, Not-Coyote was carrying a third child, with one in the tipi barely walking and another crawling. Both children were unusually mischievous, too. As Woman-Chief said, more than once, it was good her daughter-in-law was Not-Coyote, because those two certainly acted like they were Coyote's children.

Things might have gone on like this for a long time, with Not-Coyote making up stories about why her father and brothers hadn't yet come to visit (which didn't really bother anyone in the village too much, because five men — the youngest of whom killed passing grizzly bears with one skull-shattering blow — might just be offended by some of the manners in that village, and tear down the whole place and kill all the people). But Coyote hadn't planned to change himself permanently into a young woman, and so hadn't asked four times for the change. Thus, it would have been no surprise to Coyote that the change began to wear off late that fall after the third child had been born. It was, however, a great surprise to Not-Coyote, who could hardly remember Coyote at all by then.

At first the changes were small, and Not-Coyote thought maybe they were just natural for a woman with three children and a lazy husband. But then one day Not-Coyote and Stares-them-in-the-Face were being playful and chasing each other around the tipi, when one of Not-Coyote's woman parts fell off.

Stares-them-in-the-Face really stared at that. When he got his voice back, he gasped out, "You — you —" and then, as he began to understand who could do this sort of thing, he cried out, "You must be Coyote!"

Not-Coyote, who'd been looking, shocked, at the woman-part lying there on the tipi floor between them, found that the whole plan had come back to her. She changed herself once more into Coyote, threw her head back and laughed her Coyote's laugh, part laugh and part bark and howl-at-the-moon, and yelled out so everyone in the village could hear, "Yes! Stares-them-in-the-Face, your wife is Coyote! You've been married to Coyote all these years, and now you have three of Coyote's children to raise, and people will tell this story forever and laugh! They'll laugh at Stares-them-in-the-Face, who was so rude to Coyote, and they'll talk about Coyote's revenge, and no one will ever dare be rude to a guest again!"

With that, Coyote dropped to all fours and went running out of the tipi and through the camp, laughing his Coyote laugh and announcing the joke to everyone as loudly as he could. Out of the corner of one eye he saw Woman-Chief emerging from her lodge, and for a moment he almost felt badly for her. But, he thought, she should have raised her son to be polite to guests, and he didn't feel badly any more.

Then Coyote was in the hills, running and laughing, and enjoying being Coyote again. One of the things he'd forgotten during his time in Stares-them-in-the-Face's lodge was that he'd had all that trouble with his eyes, so when he changed back he had matching sharp yellow eyes, just as always. But his old eyes are still free, out there in the world looking into things they shouldn't, and sometimes they still get Coyote into trouble.

Afterword

How on earth did an Anglo come to write stories about Old
Man Coyote — the legendary American Indian Trickster,
Transformer, and Culture Hero? Part of the answer lies in my
background. I grew up in Harlem, Montana, just off the Fort
Belknap Indian Reservation, where I first knew American Indi-
ans as playmates in my own neighborhood and, soon after, as
fellow students in grade school. As I grew older, the differ-
ences between the "wild Indians" of the movies and the people
I knew in my hometown came to intrigue me more and more.
When I went off to college in 1964 I began reading about
American Indians and took some anthropology and folklore
classes.

My first encounter with Coyote came, appropriately enough,
when I took an anthropology course one summer with a professor who tended to ignore the topic and instead spent his
time telling us Coyote tales (which is probably the way Coyote
would have taught the course, too). I was hooked. I began
reading everything I could find about Coyote.

I soon discovered that Coyote wasn't the only trickster in
the world, or even in North America. Some tribes told stories

of Raven, Glooscap, or the Great Hare, for example. Europeans told stories of Reynard the Fox; Loki of Norse mythology; and Hercules of Greek myth, who tricks his way through his twelve labors. Bre'r Rabbit of the tar baby encounter is based on African folktales about a rabbit trickster; the Chinese tell tales of Monkey; and Caribbean peoples tell of Anansi the giant spider. In fact, I learned, all people everywhere tell stories of tricksters like Coyote.

While still in college, I went to work for the local Community Action Program, which included Head Start and Neighborhood Youth Corps, among other programs. That experience eventually led me back to the Fort Belknap Reservation as Director of the Community Action Program there. Seeing, as an adult, the many problems and many strengths of the Indian people led to my first two books for adults, *Buffalo and Other Stories* and *Becoming Coyote.* Later, as a graduate student at the University of Massachusetts, I took more courses in folklore and in American Indian culture. Since then, as an English professor myself, I've continued to study and even to teach a course in American Indian literature.

That's how I came to write about American Indians in general, and about Coyote in particular. Now, who is this fellow Coyote? As you can tell from the stories, he's not an ordinary coyote, but a powerful figure who can change his own shape and can also reshape the world. Yet, powerful as Coyote is, others are still more powerful. Reshaping, or changing things, is usually the most Coyote can do; he can't actually give life to anything, though he can kill — like the rest of us. For example, when Coyote calls all the animals up out of the ground, or gives life to people, it's really Earth-the-Mother who has given life. Indeed, most of the good things Coyote does come about by accident. Usually, he's just trying to get a free meal when something happens.

Like his power, Coyote's mind is also limited in some odd ways. Though he's clever — perhaps the cleverest of animals — sometimes he is so busy being clever that he outsmarts himself. The same thing is true of a popular cartoon coyote who's also probably based on Indian Coyote tales: though he hasn't got any of Old Man Coyote's magical powers, Wile E. Coyote of the Roadrunner cartoons continually outsmarts himself and falls victim to his own tricks.

Unlike Wile E. Coyote, however, our Coyote, at least in my version, doesn't have a very good memory, and he's not exactly brilliant. Coyote's tricky, and he can usually trick anyone he really wants to trick; but there's a lot he doesn't understand, especially at the start of these seven tales.

My basic conception of Coyote is based on traditional American Indian tales, and many of the incidents in these stories also come from traditional tales. At the same time, I've tried to give Coyote more personality than he's usually given. For that, I've had to draw on my own imagination: what would a character like Coyote really be like? Thus, these stories are a combination of traditional and newly imagined material.

"Coyote Learns a Lesson" offers a good example of the way in which I've developed these tales. The original tale about Coyote tricking and killing deer appears both among the Plains Indians and among the Eastern Woodlands tribes (other tribes tell a similar tale about ducks, though it doesn't involve a cliff). In the original, Coyote blindfolds deer and tricks them into dancing off a cliff. He stops only when the last living deer, a pregnant doe, convinces him to let her live so there will be more deer. The traditional story ends there.

I've added Earth-the-Mother to the story, based on other Indian stories about the Earth's fondness for dancing and the way dancing feels different to her from ordinary walking. Since she punishes him, her presence makes Coyote's lesson stronger. (The method of punishment is, I think, my own invention, though I'm not sure. I've read hundreds of traditional Coyote and trickster tales over the years, and that punishment might have occurred in one I've forgotten.)

The punishment also leads Coyote to set down some rules about how all beings should conduct themselves. Though making rules is something Coyote does in other stories, it doesn't occur in the original versions of the story about tricking the deer. (It's yet another irony about Coyote that he makes rules for others but isn't always very good about following them himself.) And though I've felt free to add to the original story, I've tried to keep the expanded version true to Indian culture and storytelling as I understand them.

This rule-making brings up an important purpose of Coyote tales: they usually teach a lesson, or perhaps more than one. Sometimes Coyote tales explain how something came to be; other times, they teach a negative lesson: don't act like that fool Coyote. Of these stories, "Coyote and Sun," "Coyote Learns a Lesson," and "Coyote's Eyes" all show ways in which people shouldn't act. On the other hand, "The Crow Buffalo-Ranchers," "Coyote's Revenge," and even the last part of "Coyote Learns a Lesson" all show Coyote setting down rules for how people should behave.

Most of all, Coyote tales are supposed to be fun, even outrageous. American Indian folktales about Coyote are among the most inventive and the funniest trickster stories in the world. I hope these stories are funny and interesting enough to fit into that tradition.